# MURDER AT THE
# HOTEL

# MURDER AT THE
# HOTEL
# HOPELESS

## JOHN LEKICH

*orca soundings*

ORCA BOOK PUBLISHERS

Published in Canada and the United States in 2022 by Orca Book Publishers.
orcabook.com

**Library and Archives Canada Cataloguing in Publication**
Title: Murder at the Hotel Hopeless / John Lekich.
Names: Lekich, John, author.
Series: Orca soundings.
Description: Series statement: Orca soundings
Identifiers: Canadiana (print) 20210366052 | Canadiana (ebook) 20210366060 |
ISBN 9781459833494 (softcover) | ISBN 9781459833500 (PDF) |
ISBN 9781459833517 (EPUB)
Subjects: LCGFT: Novels.
Classification: LCC PS8573.E498 M87 2022 | DDC jC813/.6—dc23

Library of Congress Control Number: 2021949085

**Summary:** In this high-interest accessible novel for teen readers,
an unlikely duo try to solve the murder of an international jewel thief.

Orca Book Publishers is committed to reducing the consumption
of nonrenewable resources in the production of our books. We make
every effort to use materials that support a sustainable future.

Orca Book Publishers gratefully acknowledges the support for its
publishing programs provided by the following agencies: the Government
of Canada, the Canada Council for the Arts and the Province of British
Columbia through the BC Arts Council and the Book Publishing Tax Credit.

Design by Ella Collier
Edited by Tanya Trafford
Cover photography by Getty Images/Sean Gladwell

Printed and bound in Canada.

25 24 23 22 • 1 2 3 4

*To Barbara-jo, for showing me that the best things in life happen between meals.*

# Chapter One

My name is Charlie Hope. I'm seventeen years old. I am spending the summer babysitting a celebrity named Penny Price. Something tells me this could end up being the worst summer of my life.

Penny is the star of a hit television series called *Little Miss Murder*, filming here in Vancouver. Penny Price plays Trixie Tucker. A twelve-year-old amateur detective who is a crime-solving genius.

Penny Price is only fourteen. But she thinks she knows everything. She smokes French cigarettes and eats nothing but vegetables. She says meat is very unhealthy. I made the mistake of telling her I like hot dogs. "Hot dogs will kill you, Hopeless," she said, blowing French cigarette smoke right in my face.

Hopeless. That's Penny's nickname for me. I call her Her Royal Highness, because she orders me around like she's wearing an invisible crown. She would probably do that even if she hadn't broken her right arm.

I am also taking care of Baby, Penny's little dog. Baby is a Chihuahua, and she lives in Penny's purse. Unlike Penny, Baby refuses to eat anything but steak. Which I cut up into tiny pieces for her. According to Her Royal Highness, the pieces are never tiny enough.

Penny's parents died a long time ago. Penny's official guardian is her manager, Lou Gardino. Penny calls him Hollywood Lou. He phones long distance from Los Angeles twice a day. I have to hold the phone to Penny's ear. While she uses her good arm to blow smoke in my direction. Did I mention she never says thank you?

How did I become her babysitter? Penny is hiding out at the Hotel Hope, which my mother owns. Penny calls it the Hotel Hopeless. Why? Because she cannot get a manicure or order scrambled eggs at three o'clock in the morning. Her favorite question? "Why do you not offer twenty-four-hour room service?"

Many of our tenants are pretty ancient and only watch old movies on TV. So nobody around here gets that Penny is a big star. This makes no difference to Her Royal Highness. Penny says you have to practice being famous at all times. Otherwise you forget how. And before you know it, you start acting like an ordinary person.

This is why Penny parades around the hotel lobby in her sunglasses every day. You can hear her practicing being famous all the way down the hall. "I am too busy to sign autographs today," she will say. Even when there is no one else in the lobby. Sometimes she will shout, "Help! I'm being bored to death at the Hotel Hopeless!"

I've tried to explain that the Hotel Hope is my home. I know every leaky pipe and creaky floorboard. My mother and I work hard to keep up with repairs. But the building is very old. The problem with Penny? She never listens.

There are only two ways for me to escape Penny Price. Number one? I play chess with my good friend Mr. Ignato.

Number two? I am taking driving lessons this summer. Learning how to drive makes me very nervous. But not as nervous as being around Penny. So I am driving every chance I get.

My best friend, Dexter, is teaching me how to drive. He is nineteen and has his chauffeur's license. My driving makes Dexter very nervous.

But his voice usually stays very calm. No matter how many cars I almost hit.

My problem? Penny Price. I am always thinking about Penny. Even at this very moment, when I am in the middle of a driving lesson.

Right now Dexter is telling me to switch lanes. "You will never believe what Her Royal Highness did yesterday," I said. "She made me tie her shoelace."

Dexter is Penny's number one fan. So naturally he asked, "How is her arm today?"

"Same as when you asked yesterday," I said. "Still broken."

"Do you think she'd let me sign her cast?" he asked.

Dexter's dream job? Being a celebrity limo driver for Penny Price. He has never missed an episode of *Little Miss Murder*.

"Did you see last week's show?" asked Dexter. "Trixie figured out who killed the town librarian way before the police did. You know the best part? When she squints her eyes and says, *'You're* the murderer! *Aren't* you?'"

Dexter interrupted himself to tell me to ease up on the brakes. "Relax, Charlie," he said. "You're making the tires squeal."

"You know what squealing tires remind me of?" I said. "The screeching voice of Penny Price when she is ordering me around."

We stopped at a red light. "Try to think of something nice," said Dexter. "Like getting your license and driving Lindsay Winthrop to the beach."

Lindsay Winthrop is a new tenant in our building. She is nineteen and wants to be an actress. Dexter says she is good-looking enough to be in a toothpaste commercial.

But even thinking about Lindsay's perfect teeth makes me nervous. So when the light turned green, I stepped a little too hard on the gas.

"Careful, Charlie," said Dexter. "Do you not see that old lady in the crosswalk?"

I stepped on the brake and made the tires squeal again. The old lady in the crosswalk smiled at me and waved. But Dexter said, "Driving is not bowling, Charlie. You do not get points for knocking pedestrians over."

When I said I understood, Dexter added, "That's good. Because you could scare an old lady like that to death. And my family does not need the extra business."

I should mention that Dexter's father owns the Helpful Haven Funeral Home. Dexter has been working there every summer since he was thirteen. In high school, Dexter tried to start a Future Morticians Club. I was the only guy who showed up. We've been best friends ever since.

I should also mention the kind of car I am learning to drive. It belongs to the Helpful Haven

Funeral Home. It is a hearse. Which is kind of like a limousine. Only for dead people.

Dexter's hearse is black and very long. Mostly because there has to be room for a coffin in the back. It is hard to steer around corners. Even when there is no coffin inside, it is very difficult to park.

Dexter calls his hearse "the pig." He is very fond of the pig. There is no eating or drinking allowed inside the car. Dexter knows I sweat when I get nervous. He is always afraid that I will sweat on the pig's genuine leather seats. "No sweating in the pig, Charlie!" he says. Which makes me sweat even more.

Dexter is giving me secret driving lessons. His father has no idea we are using the company car.

What would happen if I scratched or dented the pig? "My father would kill us," says Dexter. "But there is also good news. We would get a very nice funeral."

Right now a bunch of cars were honking their horns at us. Dexter made me pull over to the curb. "You're not paying attention," he said.

"Penny has ruined my concentration," I said. "Nothing has been the same since she moved into the hotel."

"No offense, Charlie," said Dexter, "but why did Penny pick your place? It is more like a rundown apartment house than a deluxe hotel. You have no fancy restaurant, and the elevator is always breaking down. Also, it is full of old people."

"Penny is hiding out," I explained. "She is avoiding reporters and photographers. They are looking for her in all the expensive hotels. But Penny says they would never bother with the Hotel Hopeless."

"I don't get why she's hiding," said Dexter.

"Her contract is up," I said. "Hollywood Lou is working out the terms of her new agreement.

Penny wants way more money from the show's producers. Lou says she has to keep hiding until they've finished negotiating. He wants her producers to think she might not come back."

"But I read somewhere that *Little Miss Murder* is still filming," said Dexter.

"They are shooting without Penny for a few days," I explained. "Because of her broken arm. But Penny says they can't last long without her."

"I still don't understand why she's hiding," said Dexter.

"If they can't find her, they can't try to make her come back," I said. "Plus she wants her producers to think she's getting other offers. You know, for movies and stuff."

"Show business sounds very complicated," said Dexter.

"Not as complicated as Penny," I said.

"Stop complaining," said Dexter. "Life could be a lot worse."

"How?" I asked. A bad question to ask anyone in the funeral business.

"Someone could die," said Dexter. "Or you could put a serious dent in the pig."

# Chapter Two

On Tuesday afternoons, I play chess with Mr. Ignato.
Mr. Ignato is seventy-five years old. He has lived
at the Hotel Hope for as long as I can remember.
Mr. Ignato has never bothered to tell me his first
name. So sometimes I like to call him Iggy.

Iggy knows pretty much everything about
me. He knows that my dad was always promising

to buy me a car one day. And how, when I was a kid, I couldn't wait to get my driver's license.

Iggy knows that my dad drove off in the middle of the night in the only car we ever had. And that he never came back.

It was Mr. Ignato who taught me how to play chess. He is an excellent chess player. He even writes down the moves for all our games in a special book. This is so he can study each game we play.

I never beat Mr. Ignato at chess. Until today. It was clear that I would soon capture his queen. Something wasn't right. "Is anything bothering you, Iggy?" I asked. "You aren't concentrating on the game."

"You're right, Charlie. Do you mind if we finish the game later?"

"Only if you tell me what's wrong," I said.

Mr. Ignato took a while to speak. "Lately I have

had the feeling that someone is watching me," he said. "But when I turn around to see who it is, nobody's there."

He looked scared. Before I could say anything, he added, "Can you keep a secret, Charlie? I'm afraid my life may be in danger."

I was so shocked by this that it took me a second to speak. "You mean someone is trying to *kill* you?" I asked.

"I don't have any proof," he answered. "It's only a feeling."

I guess I must have looked kind of upset. "I'm sorry, Charlie," Mr. Ignato said. "I must be imagining it. Forget I said anything."

"You should go to the police," I said.

"And tell them what, Charlie? I have no evidence." Mr. Ignato tried to fake a smile. "Let's talk about something else," he said. "How are things going with Penny?"

"She is still smoking," I said. "I know she is hiding those fancy cigarettes somewhere, but I can never find them. She keeps setting off the smoke alarm in her room. And her apartment is right next to mine. Sometimes *my* alarm goes off. And I can hear her shouting through the wall. 'Don't worry, Hopeless,' she yells. 'I am just frying bacon.' And she doesn't even *eat* bacon!"

"Maybe things will change when you get to know her better," said Mr. Ignato.

"I know too much about Her Royal Highness already," I replied.

"Is that a problem?" asked Mr. Ignato.

"Everything is a problem with Penny. She needs constant attention, and I'm always caught off guard. Yesterday she was wearing a new red dress. She said, 'I think this dress makes me look like a fire hydrant. What do you think, Hopeless?'"

"So?" said Mr. Ignato.

"So Penny is very short. To be honest, she *did* look a little like a fire hydrant. I didn't want to hurt her feelings, so I changed the subject. 'Speaking of fire hydrants, did you know that it is illegal to park in front of one?' But by then, Penny had stopped listening anyway. She does that a lot."

Mr. Ignato smiled for real. "How *are* your driving lessons going, anyway?"

"Not so good," I said. "This is putting a definite strain on my friendship with Dexter."

Mr. Ignato likes to keep current on my miserable social life. "How many friends do you have these days, Charlie?"

"Two," I said. "Still just you and Dexter."

"How about Penny?" asked Mr. Ignato. "Would you call her a friend?"

"No way," I replied. "Penny's only friend is her pet Chihuahua, Baby. Which makes me feel very sorry for Baby."

"Perhaps she's lonely," said Mr. Ignato.

"I doubt it," I said. "Baby gets more attention than any dog I know."

"I didn't mean Baby," said Mr. Ignato. "I meant Penny."

"But how can Penny be lonely?" I asked. "She is a big star with millions of fans."

"Everybody gets lonely," said Mr. Ignato.

"Are you ever lonely, Iggy?"

"Sometimes," he said. "But never when we play chess," he added.

I waited for him to say more. He didn't.

Mr. Ignato is a very private person. In fact, you might even call him mysterious. But I can tell when he's down. Fortunately, I know how to cheer him up. "Hey, Iggy," I said. "Can I take a look at your doorknob collection?"

"You've seen it a hundred times, Charlie," said Mr. Ignato, shaking his head. But then he smiled.

"I suppose another look wouldn't hurt."

Mr. Ignato got up to get his doorknob collection. He keeps it locked inside a wall safe that he showed to me once. It's in his bedroom, hidden behind a painting. He's the only one who knows the combination.

You may think it is strange to keep a collection of old doorknobs in a special safe. But Mr. Ignato says it's a very serious hobby and that certain doorknob collectors want his collection very badly. And they would stop at nothing to get it. I find that hard to believe. But I play along because it makes Iggy feel important. And feeling important makes him happy.

I watched Mr. Ignato walking away. He uses a cane with a silver handle in the shape of a leopard. He is never without it.

After a few minutes he returned, carrying an old leather case. He sat down like he was very glad to see the couch. Mr. Ignato unlocked the case and opened it. He began the way he always does. "Some of these doorknobs are over a hundred years old," he said. "Collectors have salvaged them from castles and mansions all over the world." I almost know the speech by heart. "Think of how many different doors they have opened, Charlie!"

The case is divided into thirty-six individual compartments for exactly that many doorknobs. Each doorknob is numbered on a carefully written label placed on the bottom edge of each compartment.

My favorite doorknob in Mr. Ignato's collection is number thirteen. At first glance it looks like a plain glass doorknob, nothing fancy. But the longer you look at it, the more it seems to sparkle.

"You're looking at number thirteen again, aren't you?" asked Mr. Ignato. "You have a good eye. It's not like the others in my collection. Number thirteen is special."

And then Mr. Ignato did something unexpected. He took number thirteen out of the case and handed it to me. "Consider this a birthday present, Charlie," he said.

"But my birthday isn't for another six months," I said.

Mr. Ignato had that scared look on his face again. "Who knows if I'm going to be around in six months?" he said. And then he added, "I'm sorry to do this to you, Charlie. But you're the most honest person I know. You're the only one I can trust with number thirteen."

"Why are you sorry for giving me a present?" I asked. "I don't understand."

"You will," said Mr. Ignato. "That's why I need you to promise me something. I want you to forgive me, Charlie. No matter what happens, please find it in your heart to forgive me."

"Forgive you for what?" I asked. "What's going to happen, Iggy?"

"Maybe nothing, Charlie," said Mr. Ignato. "Just promise."

I looked into Mr. Ignato's eyes. He wasn't just scared. He was terrified. I had no idea what was going on. And it was kind of frightening. But sometimes being a true friend means you have to have faith. And Mr. Ignato has never let me down. Not even once. So I took a chance and said, "I'll forgive you, Iggy. I promise."

"That's good, Charlie," said Mr. Ignato. "Because you know how many friends I have?"

"How many?" I asked.

"One," said Mr. Ignato, looking right at me. "Just one."

# Chapter Three

You can never push Mr. Ignato to tell you things if he doesn't want to. So that's all he said. He packed up his case and went back to his room. I figured there would always be another game of chess. I had plenty of time to ask Iggy more questions.

But I was wrong. In fact, there was no time left at all.

A few hours later I heard the scream.

It wasn't a very loud scream. But somehow I knew Iggy was in trouble. So I ran toward that horrible sound as fast as I could.

Mr. Ignato was lying at the bottom of the hotel's main staircase. Not moving at all. It was that quiet time of day when nobody else is around. There was only me and Mr. Ignato. His body all twisted in a weird position. His cane lying a few feet away. He was breathing hard.

I knelt beside him. He was trying to say something. That's when I noticed there was blood on the carpet, near his head. I yelled for help. But then I heard Mr. Ignato speak.

"Charlie?" he whispered.

"Don't talk," I said. "I'm going to call for an ambulance."

"No time," said Mr. Ignato. "Lean in closer."

And so I did.

"Mur—," he said. But he didn't finish the word.

And then he tried to say something else. But it was just too difficult. He took another ragged breath and said, "Room 22—" And then the light went out of his eyes.

He was dead.

I yelled for help again, and people started to come out of their rooms.

Later there were a couple of cars with sirens and flashing lights. Other than that, it wasn't at all like what you see on the crime shows. The investigation was over in no time. Right away, Mr. Ignato's death was officially ruled "an unfortunate accident."

They said Mr. Ignato caught his foot on the frayed carpeting, slipped and hit his head. Case closed.

Old men fall down, they said. And Iggy was just some old man who fell down for the last time. But I couldn't stop thinking about how scared he had looked earlier. I was beginning to suspect that his death was not an accident.

I even went down to the police station and talked to the desk sergeant. She told me that sometimes old people can't help imagining bad things.

I tried to talk to my mother about it. But, as usual, I picked the wrong time. She was ripping out the carpet on the main staircase. The same staircase Mr. Ignato had fallen down only days before. There were tools beside her, along with a pair of work gloves. But for some reason, she was ripping out the carpet with her bare hands. Tearing at it as hard as she could.

The main staircase is very wide and goes up a few flights. This was a huge job. So I started to help her.

"You didn't tell me you were going to start this today," I said. "I should be doing this. Anyway, where are we going to get the money for new carpeting?"

"I got another loan from the bank," she said. "We

can save some money if I rip out the old carpeting myself."

I didn't say anything. But my mother knew what I was thinking. "I know we can't afford another loan," she said.

We ripped out some more carpet together. Then my mother asked, "Are you looking after Penny?"

"I'm doing my best," I answered. "Her Royal Highness says I cut her carrot sticks too thick."

"I know Penny's difficult, Charlie. But we're being paid good money to look after her. Besides, I'm sure she appreciates having someone her own age to talk to."

"She's *not* my age," I said. "She's only fourteen." Then I noticed my mother was crying. Just ripping out carpet while the tears fell.

"I'm sorry," I told her. "I'll cut Penny's carrot sticks thinner. I promise."

But my mother wasn't crying over carrot sticks.

"That poor old man would still be alive if only I'd re-carpeted the stairs," she said.

That's when I got the crazy idea to tell my mother about my suspicions.

"What if Mr. Ignato didn't fall down the stairs?" I asked. "What if somebody *pushed* him?"

I thought this idea might make her feel a bit better. But my mother looked horrified. She stopped ripping at the carpet and stared at me. "Who would do such a terrible thing?" she asked.

"One of our tenants?" I suggested.

"What an awful thought!" she said. "Everyone who stays here is like family. They don't go around pushing their neighbors down the stairs! I don't want to hear another word about this theory of yours, Charlie."

Then my mother started tearing at the carpet again. "Don't you have a driving lesson this afternoon?" she asked.

"I don't feel like a lesson today," I said. "I'd rather help you with the stairs."

My mother put her hand on mine. She kept it there while still pulling at the carpet with her other hand. "I need to do this on my own, Charlie," she said. "Besides, you spend far too much time doing chores around here. Go have fun with Dexter."

"Driving lessons with Dexter aren't fun," I replied.

"Go anyway," she said. My mother squeezed my hand, then let go. She looked up from her work and took a deep breath. "I know Mr. Ignato was your friend," she said. "And it's sad when friends die. But there's nothing mysterious about it, Charlie. It's just part of life."

My mother asked me if I understood. I told her I did. Only because I didn't want her to start crying again. She went back to ripping up the carpet. I left to go meet Dexter for my driving lesson.

Every afternoon, Dexter takes a little nap in the pig. If there is no "customer" inside, Dexter likes to stretch out in the back. All the windows in the pig are tinted black. Nobody can see inside. Dexter finds this very restful. His favorite place to park for a nap? A quiet spot behind the hotel. And that's where I found him.

I was too upset about Iggy to actually drive. So Dexter moved up to the front seat and we stayed parked. "Sorry about your friend, Charlie," he said.

I decided to confide in Dexter about my murder theory. He told me to forget it. "According to statistics, most fatal accidents happen in the home," said Dexter. "Do you know how many old people slip on the stairs every year? All you have to do is fall a certain way. And boom, it's game over!"

Suddenly, I felt like crying. Maybe it was thinking about the way Iggy died. Or maybe that Dexter didn't believe me.

Anyway, I could feel myself getting ready to lose it. I guess that, being in the funeral business, Dexter has seen plenty of sad people. He opened the door of the pig and said, "I'm going to get us some cold drinks, okay, Charlie?"

"Okay, Dex," I said.

"You know that nobody can see inside the pig, right?" said Dexter. "All I'm saying is, it's a good place to cry in private."

"There's no crying in the pig," I said.

"There's no *sweating*, Charlie," said Dexter. "Crying is different. Everyone cries in the pig."

And so I waited for Dexter to leave. And then I cried.

It felt kind of good in a way. Until I heard a knock on the side window. The knocking wouldn't stop. So I rolled down the window. There was Penny in her red dress. Standing on the curb and looking more like a fire hydrant than ever. "I need to talk to you," she said. "I believe you, Hopeless."

"About what?" I asked.

"Murder," said Penny.

# Chapter Four

I left a note for Dexter on the windshield of the pig. Then Penny and I went back to her room at the hotel. Baby was sitting on her special cushion, looking like she wanted to escape.

The little dog was wearing a pink wool hat with knitted bunny ears. "Did you miss me, Baby?" asked Penny. "Do you like your new hat, sweetie?"

The dog looked up at me with sad eyes. They were the eyes of someone who has spent too much time trapped with Penny Price. Except for the hat, I was starting to look just like Baby.

Penny threw Baby's rubber ball. The little dog chased after the ball and brought it back. Just like she always does. It is the only thing that makes Baby truly happy. "Baby loves to play fetch so much," said Penny. "It's our favorite game, isn't it, sweetie?"

"Never mind about Baby," I said. "Why did you interrupt my driving lesson?"

"Because something isn't right about Mr. Ignato's death," said Penny. "There's a sturdy handrail on that staircase. And Mr. Ignato held on to it all the time. Plus his cane was always in his other hand for extra support."

"So?" I asked.

"So he was always very careful walking down those stairs," said Penny. "And the carpeting on that stairway has been frayed for ages. Mr. Ignato always avoided the worn patches by stepping around them. I saw him do it lots of times. Why would he fall *now*, Hopeless? Don't you find that suspicious?"

"You watched Mr. Ignato walking down the stairs?" I said.

"I watch everybody," said Penny. "As an actor, it's my duty to observe human behavior. That's how I overheard what you said to your mother on the stairs."

"You were listening in on a private conversation with my mother?" I asked. "Why didn't I see you?"

"Don't you ever watch my show?" asked Penny. "You weren't *supposed* to see me. I was on a stakeout. You know what a stakeout is, right? That's when a private investigator follows someone around without them noticing. You know, to get valuable information for a case."

"I don't care what you call it," I said. "It's not polite to listen in on private conversations."

"There is nothing polite about investigating a murder," said Penny. She sounded just like the character she plays on her show. And then Penny said, "Back there in the car. You were crying, weren't you?"

"That is none of your business," I said.

"There's no shame in crying, Hopeless," said Penny. "But from now on, you're going to control your emotions. We have a crime to solve. Since I've broken my arm, you're going to be my faithful assistant."

"*Faithful assistant*? What do I have to do?" I asked.

"Whatever I say," answered Penny. "Like opening the envelopes of secret messages. Or opening the door to a hidden tunnel. Things like that."

"You just want me around to *open* stuff?" I asked.

"Exactly," said Penny. "Don't worry, Hopeless. I'll do all the thinking."

"You really think you can solve Mr. Ignato's murder?" I asked.

"Why not?" said Penny. "I've solved dozens of murders."

"On your show!" I said. "Pretend murders don't count."

"Sure they do," said Penny. "You know the only difference between a real murder and one on a crime show?" she asked. "At work, the dead body gets up for a sandwich when we break for lunch. But the same basic rules of investigation apply in real life."

"What rules?" I asked.

"First we need to find a motive," she explained. "*Why* would somebody want to kill a harmless old man? Then we need to find evidence. Clues that point the way to our killer."

"So you do all the investigating," I said. "And I just hang around to open the secret envelope. What if there isn't a secret envelope?"

"Trust me," said Penny. "There's always a secret envelope."

"Why is this so important to you, anyway?" I asked.

"I told you, Hopeless," said Penny. "I used to watch Mr. Ignato. There was something mysterious about him. His clothes, for example. They're very old but also very expensive. Why is an elegant man like that living in your dreary little hotel?"

Before I could answer, Penny said, "I'll *tell* you why. He's hiding something! Something from his past. Let's find out what it is, Hopeless."

That's how I ended up using my master key to enter Mr. Ignato's apartment. My mother gave me a copy for my seventeenth birthday. She made me promise to only use it for emergencies.

I figured this was an emergency. Still, it felt kind of weird being there without Mr. Ignato. It felt even weirder being there with Penny.

"Look around for a clue, Hopeless," she commanded. "Sometimes if a person suspects they're in danger, they leave a hidden clue. Something important that only their best friend could find."

"Why do you think real life is anything like the movies?" I asked. "This is not an episode of *Little Miss Murder*."

"What's that note on the desk?" asked Penny. "The yellow one."

That's when I noticed Iggy's special notebook. The one he used to record the moves in all our chess games. There was a yellow note stuck on the front cover.

It read, *Charlie, sorry we couldn't finish our last game. Wondering what your next move should be? Check out the last page in my notebook. You will find a safe opening strategy in my final move.*

I could feel Penny reading over my shoulder. "I don't play chess," she said. "But a safe opening strategy? That's a series of moves at the *beginning* of the game, right?"

When I nodded, she asked, "So how can you find a safe opening strategy in a final move? A final move is at the very *end* of the game. It doesn't make sense."

I turned to the last chess move written in Mr. Ignato's notebook. But it wasn't in the familiar code all chess players use for recording games. "His last entry looks different from the others," said Penny.

"That's because it has nothing to do with chess," I said. "It's not a safe opening strategy. It's a strategy for *opening a safe*. This is the combination to Mr. Ignato's wall safe!"

We went to Mr. Ignato's bedroom. I showed Penny his safe. I tried the combination, and it worked! I pulled open the heavy door.

"Look for the secret envelope," said Penny.

There was a bunch of stuff inside. But the first thing we noticed was a large brown envelope. There was writing on the outside of the envelope. *For Charlie Hope. To Be Opened After My Murder.*

I just stood there, staring at the word *murder*.

"What are you waiting for, Hopeless?" asked Penny. "Do I have to do *everything*?"

# Chapter Five

The envelope contained an old VCR tape. I only knew what it was because Mr. Ignato still had an old-school player that he'd taught me how to use a long time ago. We used to watch tapes of famous chess games together.

I put the tape in the machine and turned it on. There was Mr. Ignato on the screen of his ancient television set. Sitting in his favorite chair, with his cane by his side, Mr. Ignato began to speak slowly, pausing often for breath.

"*Hello, Charlie,*" he said. "*I made this tape a few days ago, in case something happens to me. By the way, congratulations for discovering the combination to my safe. All those games of chess have taught you well, Charlie. And you're going to need to keep thinking a few moves ahead.*"

Then Mr. Ignato leaned forward in his chair. "*By now, you must know I'm dead,*" he said. "*And it was no accident. Someone has murdered me. But I'm getting ahead of my story. The first thing you have to know? My real name is not Mr. Ignato. I had to change it. Why? Because I've done some bad things, Charlie.*"

Mr. Ignato kept talking. "*Many years ago I was once a very famous burglar. They called me the Leopard. Because I was so quick and so quiet that nobody could catch me.*"

Iggy leaned forward even closer. "*I stole many valuable things,*" he said. "*But as I grew older, I came* to regret my life of crime. The word Ignato means 'nothing' or 'zero' in Italian. My new name was a private joke to myself. Because my past life as a thief made me feel so worthless and ashamed."

Then Mr. Ignato smiled. "But it wasn't always that way, Charlie. You know my doorknob collection? Every single doorknob is from a place I robbed. A little souvenir to remember each of my criminal adventures."

Iggy paused. He looked like he was remembering the good old days.

Penny was busy looking up some information on her phone. "The Leopard was famous all over the world," she said. "Stealing doorknobs from the scene of the crime was his trademark."

Mr. Ignato began to speak again. "One day the police caught me and put me in an American jail. My only friend was my cellmate. A man named Sam Logan, who was serving a life sentence."

"*After I was released from prison, I used to write Sam often. I told him all about you and my life at the hotel, Charlie. Sam was the only one who knew my secret. The secret that has killed me.*"

Penny and I waited. But Iggy said nothing for a couple of minutes. We watched as he took out his doorknob collection and opened the case. And then he said, "*I don't know who has murdered me, Charlie. But I know the reason why. Number thirteen.*"

"What's number thirteen?" asked Penny.

"A doorknob," I said. "From Iggy's collection."

Mr. Ignato took number thirteen out of his case. "*Now, Charlie,*" he said. "*Watch very closely. I always told you that number thirteen was special. And you're about to find out why.*"

Mr. Ignato brought his hands close to the screen. Now we could see the doorknob close up. He turned it over to give us a good look at the bottom.

"*Pay close attention, Charlie,*" said Iggy. "*This may look like an ordinary doorknob. But I had it specially altered by a master clockmaker in Switzerland.*"

Penny and I watched the old man's hands. "*There's a little switch at the bottom here,*" he said. "*It looks just like a typical screw. But when you turn the screw a certain way? It triggers a hidden spring. It's a little tricky at first. But you'll get the hang of it. Now watch. Pull the screw halfway out. Turn it left once, then right, then left again. Like so.*"

Suddenly the top of the doorknob sprung open. Now number thirteen didn't look like a doorknob at all. It looked like a small box that opened on a hinge. The glass top of the doorknob formed a lid. The bottom part of the doorknob was the rest of the box.

Iggy didn't say a word. He held the box so we could see the treasure it contained. I was lost for words. I heard Penny say, "That's the biggest diamond I've ever seen in my life!"

The old man took the large diamond out of its doorknob case. He held it in his hand and began to talk again. "*This is the Countess Grazelli diamond,*" he said. "*Known the world over as the Countess. It was once one of Italy's national treasures. Hundreds of years old and worth well over a million dollars. By far the most precious gem I ever stole.*

"*I know what you what you're thinking, Charlie,*" he added. "*Why didn't I sell the Countess?*"

Iggy sighed. "*I didn't sell it because there's a curse on the diamond,*" he explained. "*Whoever owns it will have a lifetime of bad luck. Or worse, no life at all.*"

Iggy looked very grim. "*You can research the tragic history of the Countess for yourself, Charlie,*" he continued. "*You will soon learn that many of the diamond's previous owners have been murdered.*

The curse certainly applied to me. I spent years in prison. I lost all my money and all my friends."

The old man put the Countess back in its secret hiding place and snapped the case shut. Number thirteen was back to being a doorknob again. "*I made a decision after getting out of prison,*" said Iggy. "*I wasn't going to pass that bad luck on to someone else. Even if it meant the curse of the Countess would kill me someday. So I kept the diamond all these years. Waiting for the curse toend my life.*

"*But then I got to thinking,*" he added. *There's probably a big reward for the return of the diamond. That reward could mean a better future for you and your mother, Charlie. So, I decided to take the risk and pass the diamond on to you. I hope I did the right thing. Because now the risk is all yours, Charlie.*"

I could tell Iggy was getting tired. But he kept on talking anyway. "*There's something you need to know. Only one person knew I had the Countess, Charlie. My former cellmate. But Sam died in prison last year. So I don't know who could have killed me. But someone has. And it's all about the diamond."*

The old man stopped talking to rest for a few seconds. Then he said, *"I don't know what you did with the Countess, Charlie. But I am sorry. I thought someone as clever as you might figure out a way to avoid or end the curse. It's your responsibility now. Just don't put it back in my safe. If someone is watching you, that's the first place they'll look. And I wouldn't want anybody blowing up your hotel trying to get it open. Many criminals are as desperate as they are greedy. And the desperate ones are always the most dangerous. Remember that, Charlie."*

I heard Penny ask, *"You have the diamond, Hopeless?"*

But Iggy started to speak again before I could answer. *"I can't tell you what to do with the Countess, Charlie. I know the money from the diamond could make your mother's life so much easier. But I'm counting on you to do the right thing. Turn it in to the police. The Countess is nothing but trouble."*

Iggy looked very sad. "*Thank you for being my friend, Charlie,*" he said. "*I'd forgotten what friendship was like until you came along. And while we're on the subject? Try to be nicer to Penny. Something tells me you're going to need all the friends you can get.*"

Mr. Ignato tried to smile. "*Don't forget your promise, Charlie,*" he said. "*Forgive an old man for his weakness. And one last thing. Good luck on your driving test, son.*"

And then the screen went blank.

I just sat there. Thinking about all the things Iggy had said. After a while I turned to Penny. "Can you believe it?" I asked.

But she didn't answer. When she finally spoke, her voice was suspiciously sweet.

"Charlie?" she asked. "Where did you hide the Countess?"

# Chapter Six

"I haven't got the Countess, Penny," I said. I was lying, of course. Something I almost never do. Because I am a very bad liar.

So why did I lie? I didn't have a lot of time to waste arguing with Her Royal Highness. Number thirteen—the doorknob that contained the Countess—was in my room. Sitting on my desk. I was using a million-dollar diamond as a paperweight.

I needed to get away from Penny to hide the diamond somewhere safe. But Penny wouldn't let me go. She went all Trixie Tucker on me. "You're lying to me, Hopeless," she said.

I could see that Penny was not going to give up. "Okay, I have the diamond," I said. "But I'm going to turn it over to the police. Like Mr. Ignato told me to."

"So I guess you don't want to catch your friend's killer," said Penny. "Don't you see, Hopeless? We need to use the diamond as bait. To lure the killer out into the open."

"That sounds too dangerous," I said. "Hanging on to the diamond will make both of us targets for the murderer."

"You're forgetting one thing," said Penny. "I've spent four years playing Trixie Tucker. The greatest detective on network television. The killer can't do anything that I haven't seen a hundred times."

"I know one thing you haven't seen," I said.

"What's that, Hopeless?" asked Penny.

"That the killer can actually *kill* us," I said. "For real! No phony blood. No fake bullets. And no stuntman to fall down the stairs for you. Plus you're forgetting about the curse of the Countess."

Penny looked at me with disgust. "You don't actually believe that fairy tale about a curse, do you, Hopeless?"

"I just did some quick computer research on the history of the Countess," I said. "People who have the diamond keep dying. One guy got run over by an ice-cream truck! Besides, why are you so interested in keeping the diamond? You have plenty of money."

"Imagine the publicity I'll get when I solve a real case," said Penny. "Everyone will want to watch my show."

"You make it sound so easy," I said.

"It is, Hopeless," said Penny. "I'll make you a deal. If we can find enough proof to convince the police of murder? We'll turn in the evidence *and* the diamond at the same time. All you have to do? Hang on to the Countess long enough for us to investigate."

"Okay," I said. "But I'm hiding the diamond myself. And I'm not going to tell you where it is." It suddenly occurred to me that this was an opportunity to make some other demands. "Also you have to let my friend Dexter sign your cast," I added. "Plus you have to stop smoking. Before you burn down the entire hotel."

"Fair enough," said Penny. "I accept your terms, Hopeless. Now let's get to work. You were the last person to see Mr. Ignato alive. Did he tell you anything?"

I told Penny what Mr. Ignato had said before he died. How he got halfway to the word *murder* before trying to say a room number at the hotel.

Penny got excited. "Who lives in room 22?" she asked.

"There *is* no room 22," I said. "But there are several rooms that begin with those two numbers.

Mr. Ignato died before he could finish saying the whole room number."

"So all we have to do is check out each of the apartments that begin with 22," said Penny. "One of those tenants must know something about the murder."

"What are we supposed to do?" I asked. "Knock on people's doors? And say, 'Excuse me. Have you pushed anybody down the stairs lately?'"

"You leave that to me," said Penny. "In the meantime? There must be one or two tenants we can cross off our list of suspects."

"There's Mrs. Kent in 225," I said. "She's in a wheelchair. There's no way she could push anyone down the stairs."

Penny narrowed her eyes. "Are you sure she's not faking it?" she asked.

"What kind of person fakes being in a wheelchair?" I asked.

"A murderer, that's who," said Penny. "We should

check out the bottoms of her shoes for scuff marks. If it looks like she's been walking in them, she could be our killer."

"Let me guess," I said. "You got that from an episode of *Little Miss Murder.*"

"Are you going to take this seriously or not?" asked Penny.

"Mrs. Kent has arthritis," I said. "Plus she has a heart condition."

"What's your point, Hopeless?"

"I know everyone in the building," I said. "The closest thing we have to a criminal is Mr. Gilroy. Sometimes he grabs Mrs. Penski's newspaper before she can collect it from the hallway."

"So you're saying we shouldn't investigate the tenants?" asked Penny.

"No," I said. "I'm only saying that nobody knows the hotel guests better than I do. You have to start trusting my judgment."

Penny thought about this. "Okay," she said. "I'll try my best, Hopeless. But I can't make any promises."

Penny decided to take Baby for her daily walk. That gave me a chance to hide the diamond. I thought, Why not take advantage of the fact that it is inside a doorknob?

I'm pretty handy at basic home repairs. You have to be when you live at the Hotel Hope. So it was no problem for me to substitute one doorknob for another.

I went down to a small storage closet in the basement of the hotel. The closet is full of old junk, and nobody uses it anymore. But you can lock the closet door with an old key. I unscrewed the old doorknob on the inside of the closet door. Replacing it with number thirteen.

At first I was afraid number thirteen would be too heavy to fit the doorknob hole. But everything fit just fine. I could turn the ordinary knob on the outside of the storage closet and open the door. Number thirteen turned on the inside of the door at the same time. And it wasn't visible unless the door was wide open.

I locked the door of the storage closet and tried to forget about the diamond. But trying to forget about the Countess was like trying to forget about Penny. We were stuck with each other, whether we liked it or not. And I couldn't help wondering what awful thing was going to happen next.

For several days nothing happened.

But every night I had the same bad dream about somebody stealing the Countess. Somebody in the shadows, who I couldn't see. Waiting to push me down the stairs.

Every day I went to check on the Countess. To make sure it was still where I'd left it.

It was always deserted in the hotel basement. But I kept looking over my shoulder. Because I was sure somebody was watching me.

I told myself I was just making sure Penny didn't follow me. But it wasn't Penny who worried me.

It was whoever had killed Mr. Ignato. And I had to find out who. Before they figured out that I was the one looking after the Countess.

# Chapter Seven

Penny and I agreed to check out the tenants in rooms beginning with "22." We made a list of the six apartments and divided it up between us. Penny wore a red wig because she didn't want anybody to recognize that she was a famous celebrity. "Today I am playing a brand new role," she said. "A humble redhead who thinks only of others."

"This will be a refreshing change for both of us," I replied.

Then Penny did something that surprised me. She laughed. "Sometimes you can be quite amusing, Hopeless," she said. "But this is no time for jokes. We have a murder to solve."

Penny told the three tenants on her list that she was collecting for charity. She didn't find any suspects. But she collected seven dollars and fifty cents. I made her put it into the fund for the annual hotel Christmas party.

I helped Mrs. Lenowski in 226 get a can of tomato sauce off her top shelf. And changed a light bulb for Mr. Durham in 227. But neither one of them confessed to murder.

I must admit that I was a bit nervous knocking on the door of 222A. This is where Lindsay Winthrop has lived for the past month or so. The same Lindsay I think about driving to the beach. Once I get my license.

Room 222A is a very small apartment. It used to be just plain 222. And much bigger back in the day. But then my mother split the old 222 in half to make another smaller suite. Which is now called 222B. There is still a connecting door between the two apartments. Which usually stays locked.

The thing about Lindsay? She never complains about her apartment being too small. Or why she has to put up with a connecting door to 222B that's always locked. I should find her easy to talk to. But our conversations are usually very short.

Every time I see Lindsay in the hallway, she smiles at me, and I try to smile back. She always says, "Hello, Charlie." And I always answer, "Hello, Ms. Winthrop."

But I have never knocked on Lindsay Winthrop's door before. I had to knock twice. I was starting to sweat. And I wasn't even driving the pig. I was kind of hoping Lindsay wouldn't answer the door. But she did.

"Hello, Charlie," said Lindsay. "This is a nice surprise." She smiled at me. Her smile was dazzling like always.

I guess Lindsay was waiting for me to say something. But what? I could not bring myself to ask her if she killed Mr. Ignato. Or tell her about all the troubles in my life. Who would believe I was babysitting Penny Price *and* a cursed, million-dollar diamond?

Lindsay kept smiling and waiting for me to speak. Finally I said, "I'm just checking. To see if anything in your apartment needs fixing."

"I can't think of anything," said Lindsay. "But I'd appreciate your checking the apartment right next to me."

"222B?" I asked. "That apartment is empty right now."

"Didn't your mother tell you?" asked Lindsay. "My uncle Ned is coming to visit me for a few weeks. He's decided to rent it. So we'll be right next to each other. I was wondering if you could make sure to unlock the connecting door between our apartments. My uncle has some health problems. And I want to keep a close eye on him."

"Sure, Ms. Winthrop," I said. "We do that all the time for close relatives."

"Thanks, Charlie. There is something else you can do for me," she said.

"Oh? What's that?"

"Please call me Lindsay."

"Okay, Ms.—I mean, Lindsay," I said. I could feel the sweat dripping down my shirt.

"Would you like to come in for a glass of water, Charlie?" asked Lindsay. "You look a little warm."

"No, thank you," I said. I didn't want to tell her I was busy checking out murder suspects. So I added, "I have a driving lesson in a few minutes."

"Well, good luck," she said with another big smile. "Drop by anytime. It's always nice to see you."

"Nice to see you too, Lindsay," I replied. But I don't think she heard me. Because, by the time I said it, the door was already closed. I was actually kind of relieved. At least she didn't get to see the drop of sweat sliding down my nose.

During my driving lesson, I really wanted to concentrate. But Dexter was way more interested in my meeting with Lindsay. "So let me get this straight," he said. "She invited you in for a glass of water, and you *didn't* go inside?"

"I wasn't thirsty," I explained.

Dexter looked disgusted. "Who cares if you were thirsty? Maybe she likes you, Charlie."

"Why?" I asked. "I don't even have my driver's license."

Trying to do a lesson that day turned out to be a very big mistake. I felt even more weird behind the wheel than usual. I figured it was all the talk about Lindsay liking me. I thought I'd be okay once I started driving.

I wasn't.

Before the Countess, my nightmares were all about crashing the pig. In my car-crash nightmares, everything happened in slow motion. A lot like how it happened in real life.

But in real life it was worse. Everything was going okay until I swerved to avoid hitting a cat that had darted into traffic. The cat got away without a scratch. But not the pig.

I guess I turned too hard to the right. The front end of the pig ended up on the sidewalk. It hit a nearby trash bin, and a whole bunch of paper coffee cups and fast-food wrappers spilled all over the place.

We got out to inspect the damage. There was a big dent on the front of the pig. I tried to apologize to Dexter, but he wasn't talking to me.

I found out later that Dexter took the blame for the accident. And that his dad took away his pig privileges. For a while Dexter was stuck working in the Helpful Haven showroom. Helping future dead people plan ahead.

I went to the funeral home to talk to Dexter. He was in the showroom, talking to a man lying in a coffin. "How does it feel?" Dexter asked him. "Comfortable, right?" I figured some people like to take their final resting places for a test drive.

Dexter looked cranky and tired. I wondered if he was missing his afternoon naps in the pig. When he saw me, he said, "Go away, Charlie. I am busy with a live customer."

I said I needed to talk to him.

"Are you here to discuss plans for your funeral, Charlie?" asked Dexter. "If so, I will be more than happy to assist you. But if it's for anything else, don't bother. From now on, you are dead to me."

The man lying in the coffin sat up. "Is this a bad time?" he asked. "I can come back later."

But it was no use. I had lost my only friend. And driving lessons were clearly over. I felt bad about the whole thing. I thought it would help if I went to Dexter's dad and took the blame for denting the pig. But it only made Dexter more angry. I decided I'd just have to give him some space.

Back at the hotel, Penny was very upset. Her manager had called and told her some bad news. "My producers think I'm getting too tall to play a twelve-year-old," she explained.

"But you're the shortest person I know," I said.

"That's sweet, Hopeless," said Penny. "But let's face it, I'm not getting any younger. The whole point of *Little Miss Murder* is that she's *little*. Little and *cute*. That's why people watch. The producers say they'll replace me with a ten-year-old if I refuse to come back. A ten-year-old! That's four whole years younger than me!"

"What about your broken arm?" I asked.

"They are writing my broken arm into the next storyline," said Penny.

"So what's the problem?" I said. "Go back to work."

"If I go back to work, they are going to pay me way *less*," she said.

Penny began waving around a magazine called *Secrets of the Stars*. "There is a terrible story about me in here. It's even worse online. They are calling me a selfish, spoiled brat. I will sue them!"

"Can you sue them if it's true?" I asked. The words were out of my mouth before I could stop them.

"Don't you understand, Hopeless?" said Penny. "My producers planted the story. They are putting pressure on me to come back. I won't do it!"

After that things kept getting worse. My mother got a notice from the bank. It said we had sixty days to make the back payments for our mortgage. Otherwise the bank would take over ownership of the hotel.

It seemed like the curse of the Countess was working its magic. I went down to the basement to check on the diamond. I unlocked the storage closet, opened the door and unscrewed number thirteen. I opened the case and was shocked to see that it was gone.

# Chapter Eight

I am no detective. But I'd watched enough episodes of *Little Miss Murder* to ask myself one question. What would Trixie Tucker do?

Trixie would go straight to the only other person who knew about the diamond. Penny Price.

I was going to ask about the diamond right away. But I was distracted by the red wig Penny wore. It sat crookedly on her head and looked like it was going to fall off.

I had to ask. "Why are you still wearing that stupid wig, Penny?"

"If you must know, my hair is falling out in clumps," she said.

Then she dramatically pulled a cigarette from her purse. "Would you light my cigarette, Hopeless? I can't do it with this hand." She pulled out a lighter too and handed it to me.

"You promised to stop smoking," I said. "Where did you get that cigarette?"

"I'll never tell," said Penny. "It's a secret."

I guess Penny could tell I was upset. "I know I promised to stop smoking, Hopeless," she added. "But this is a cigarette emergency! I am super-stressed. And I need to calm my nerves."

"Smoking is not allowed inside the hotel," I said. "Also, it is very bad for your health. Also, you are too young and it is illegal. Also, you could start a fire!"

"It helps me relax," said Penny. "Are you going to light my cigarette or not? If not, I will be moving out of here tomorrow. That means Hollywood Lou will stop paying my rent."

I lit Penny's cigarette. I started to cough from the smoke.

I looked at Penny's good arm. The one holding her precious cigarette. "What are those little red bumps?" I asked.

"Hives," said Penny. "It must be some kind of allergy. It itches like crazy."

"Don't you see?" I asked. "The rash, your hair. It's the curse! You have the Countess, don't you, Penny?"

Penny looked at me. "Of course I have the diamond, Hopeless," she said. "And I have hidden it where nobody else can find it. Just like my cigarettes."

"But *I* hid the Countess," I said. "And I locked the storage closet."

"I followed you when you hid the diamond," said Penny. "Then when nobody was in the basement? I picked the lock of the storage closet."

"What?" I said. "You *picked* the lock?"

"Don't look so surprised, Hopeless," said Penny. "Someone on the show taught me how to do it with a hairpin. And the closet has a very old lock."

"But you promised not to follow me," I said.

"I'm sorry, Hopeless," said Penny. "But that diamond is my future. Lou just had a meeting with the producers of my show. They are bringing in Trixie Tucker's ten-year-old cousin Teri." She got out her phone and showed me a picture of the actress replacing her. "Look, Hopeless," said Penny. "She is ten years old and cuter than Baby!"

"What has any of this got to do with the Countess?" I asked.

"If I get fired?" said Penny. "I'm going to need the money from the diamond to start my own production company. Then I can be my own boss.

I know someone in Hollywood who'll buy the Countess. No questions asked."

"But you're rich," I said. "Why do you need the diamond?"

Penny sighed. "Lou handles all my money," she said. "He's made some bad investments. I'm almost *poor*, Hopeless. I can't *do* poor. Don't worry. We'll split the profits. I heard about the bank taking over ownership of your hotel. This way you can pay off the mortgage."

"With the profits from selling a stolen diamond?" I said. "My mother would disown me." And then I remembered the curse. "I have wrecked the pig and lost my best friend. I will never get my driver's license. All because I am babysitting a priceless jewel I don't even want."

"I don't care," said Penny. "You are not going to force me to live on a budget, Hopeless. And what about poor Baby? Do you expect her to eat bargain dog food?"

"I thought we were keeping the diamond to trap Mr. Ignato's murderer," I said.

"We're going to have to put the investigation on hold," said Penny. "I'm much too upset about my career."

I'd had enough of Her Royal Highness. "That's it," I said. "I quit! Keep the diamond. But if I were you, I'd turn it in to the police."

For the next few days, I stayed far away from Penny. It was almost like taking a vacation in Hawaii. The funny thing is, Penny did not move out of her apartment. She didn't even complain to my mother.

At the same time, my luck started to change for the better. I met Lindsay Winthrop's uncle Ned when he was moving into 222B.

Ned was a little guy with big glasses. He looked like a high-school science teacher. But it turned out he was a real-estate developer. He even gave me his business card. Then you know what he said? "You and Lindsay make a cute couple."

Before long Lindsay and I were showing Ned all around Vancouver. The three of us went on picnics and to museums and restaurants. It was a lot of fun.

But you want to know the best part? Lindsay agreed to give me driving lessons in her uncle Ned's sports car. I told her how I had crashed the pig. But she didn't seem to mind at all.

It turned out Lindsay was the exact opposite of Penny Price. She was very interested in my life. I told her all about how Penny and Baby were driving me crazy. I even told her how my mother might lose the hotel. And how I was very worried about it.

That's when Ned told me a secret over lunch. "I'm considering buying your hotel, Charlie. I have some investors lined up who want to go into partnership with your mother."

Ned's plan? Pay off our debts and renovate the entire place.

Ned made me promise not to tell my mother yet. He needed to look around the hotel a bit more. "To see if it is the right fit for our investors."

I offered to show him around the hotel. And pretty soon Ned knew the place almost as well as I did.

Every once in a while, I saw Penny and Baby in the hallway. I even introduced the two of them to Lindsay and Ned. Just to be polite. All Penny said to Lindsay was, "Hopeless is more sensitive than he looks. Please do not break his heart."

Things were going pretty well. In fact, I had almost forgotten about the curse of the Countess. Then there was a fire in Penny's room. In the middle of the night. By the time I got there, you could smell the smoke and hear Baby barking.

The smoke alarm was whining. And Penny was using the fire extinguisher from the hallway to put out a cigarette fire in her wastebasket.

Penny tried to convince me that she hadn't started the fire. "Do you think I'd be stupid enough to use a wastebasket for an ashtray?" she asked. "Besides, I never smoke at night. And *you* have to light my cigarettes, remember?"

"If it wasn't you, who was it?" I asked. "How did they get in your room?"

"I don't know," said Penny. "It was dark, and I was asleep. But somebody got into my room and started the fire. They got away before I woke up. You believe me, don't you, Hopeless?"

"Why can't you admit you made a mistake?" I said. "Don't you understand? This place is my home. And it's home to a lot of other people too. I know you think it's just some broken-down old dump. But I never thought even you could be *this* selfish."

After that I walked away. As I turned my back, I could hear Penny's voice. "Charlie!" she shouted. "I didn't do it!"

A couple of days later, Penny knocked on my door.

"I don't want to talk to you right now, Penny," I said.

"Listen, Charlie," she said. "Someone has searched my room. They've gone through all my things."

"Did they find the Countess?" I asked.

"No," said Penny. "But I can tell they looked everywhere."

"Didn't you lock your door?" I asked.

"Of course I did," said Penny. "Someone has made a copy of your master key. They can get into any apartment they want."

"That's impossible," I said. "Only two people have copies of the master key. My mother and me."

"It's not impossible," said Penny. "I know who has another copy."

"Who?" I asked.

Penny looked at me. Her face all blotchy with hives. Her red wig still crooked. "The same person who started the fire in my room," she said. "The same person who murdered Mr. Ignato. Do you want to know who it is?"

# Chapter Nine

"You know who murdered Mr. Ignato?" I asked.

"Yes. I'm pretty sure it's Lindsay's uncle, Ned," said Penny. "Or maybe even Lindsay. Or they planned it together."

"So you *don't* know. Anyway, that doesn't make any sense," I said. "Why would they want to kill Iggy?"

"They want the Countess, Hopeless," said Penny. "I even figured out how Lindsay could have made a copy of your master key. She made a wax impression of the key's shape. That's all you need to make an exact copy of the key."

"Let me guess," I said. "Another thing you learned from your show."

"Good guess, Hopeless," said Penny. "I'll bet that's exactly how Lindsay did it." Her Royal Highness looked very pleased with herself. Then she added, "Haven't you wondered why Lindsay is so interested in you?"

"What do you mean by that?" I asked.

"I mean Lindsay looks like a fashion model," said Penny. "Plus she's two whole years older than you. No offense, Hopeless, but you've had the same peanut butter stain on your shirt since yesterday. And half the time you don't even bother to comb your hair. Don't you find her sudden attraction to you just a little suspicious?"

I guess I should have felt insulted. But, to be completely honest, I had wondered the same thing myself. I avoided the subject altogether. "You can't go around accusing innocent people of murder, Penny. You need proof, remember?"

"Let's see your master key, Hopeless. There could still be a trace of wax on it."

I took the master key off my keychain. I got a magnifying glass and looked closely at the key. There was a small trace of wax on it.

"Now think, Hopeless," said Penny. "Did you ever leave Lindsay alone with your keys? During a driving lesson maybe?"

"The other day I went to get us a couple of coffees," I said. "My keys were in the pocket of my jacket."

"And you left your jacket in the car, right?" said Penny.

"Yes," I said. "But I was only gone a couple of minutes."

"Whose idea was it to get coffee?" asked Penny. "Lindsay's?"

I nodded. "I don't even drink coffee."

"There's more, Hopeless," said Penny. "I've just been on the longest stakeout of my life. I saw Ned go into Mr. Ignato's room. Using a key."

"But we haven't rented Iggy's room," I said. "All his stuff is still in there."

"Exactly," said Penny. "I *saw* him use a key to go in. Then he came out about an hour later. He was looking for the Countess."

"But Ned is a real-estate developer," I said. "He showed me his business card."

"What does that mean? Anyway, anyone can have a fake business card made up," said Penny. "And pretending to be a real-estate agent? It's the perfect excuse to check out the entire hotel."

"There's something else," I said. "Isn't there?"

"Ned went into your apartment next," said Penny. "I saw him. Did you notice anything different in your room? Anything out of place?"

"No," I said. "But my room's always a mess."

"You know something, Hopeless?" said Penny. "Sometimes you really *are* hopeless."

"Well, excuse me for not being like the great Trixie Tucker," I said. "But neither are you. *You* saw Ned going into my apartment. Why didn't you say something? Why didn't you stop him?"

I waited for Penny to answer. She looked uncomfortable. "I wanted to stop him," she said finally. "But I was scared."

Penny reached into her purse with her good hand. She put a crumpled cigarette to her lips. "Don't worry, Hopeless. I'm not going to light it. It just makes me feel better."

I took a long look at Penny Price. Her wig had slipped down the front of her forehead, which was dotted with hives. And that tired-looking cigarette drooping from her mouth. She was a mess. I was actually beginning to feel sorry for her.

But I wasn't much better. I couldn't believe I'd let Lindsay trick me to copy my master key. "I guess I have been pretty hopeless," I said, "haven't I?"

"Don't worry, Charlie," said Penny, letting the cigarette fall out of her mouth. "I have a plan."

Penny explained that somehow we had to get Ned and Lindsay out of their apartments. Then we could search both places for evidence. Using my master key. "When we have enough proof, we'll go to the police with the diamond," said Penny.

"You mean it this time?" I asked.

"I swear on Baby's life," said Penny. "And there's nobody more important to me than Baby."

That's how Penny, Baby and I ended up searching Ned and Lindsay's apartments. First Penny phoned them both, disguising her voice. She told them she had the Countess and that if they wanted it, they should meet her at the Hotel Vancouver.

Ned and Lindsay would have to drive all the way downtown and back. This would give us enough time to search for evidence to give the police.

It was Penny who found Lindsay's diary. It had a lock that secured a leather strap in place. You couldn't open the book without a key. But Penny picked the lock with a hairpin.

It turned out there was good news and bad news. The good news? Lindsay kind of liked me after all. That's why she felt so guilty about what she was doing.

The bad news? Ned was not Lindsay's uncle. Ned had hired Lindsay to spy on me. And gain my trust and find out where the diamond was. *Ned is sure that Charlie has hidden the Countess somewhere*, she wrote.

It was clear by the words she'd written that she was starting to panic. She even wondered if Ned had pushed Iggy down the stairs.

I looked at Penny. "We need to take this to the police."

"The diary isn't enough," said Penny. "There are still too many questions. How does Ned know about the diamond? Why does he think you have it? We need to find the connection between Mr. Ignato and Ned, Charlie."

"You think we should still try to search Ned's room?" I asked. I looked at my watch. "We don't have much time before they get back."

"So let's be quick," said Penny. "I'm really hoping we find something in Ned's room that we can use."

And we did. Hidden under some papers was a picture of Ned and another man. They were both wearing prison uniforms. But the other man was not Mr. Ignato.

"Turn the photo over," I said. "Maybe there's writing on the back."

Penny turned over the photo. "Nice work, Hopeless," she said. "It says 'Me and Sam Logan.'"

"That was Mr. Ignato's friend."

"That's the connection, Charlie!" said Penny. "Sam Logan was a cellmate of both Ned and Mr. Ignato."

"Now can we go to the police?" I asked.

That's when I heard a voice behind us. "I wouldn't do that, Charlie."

Ned was standing there with Lindsay in the open doorway. "We were almost downtown when I realized this had to be a diversion. You are the only person who could have the diamond, Charlie. I'm done with making foolish mistakes." He looked at Lindsay. She closed the door and locked it.

Penny and I just stood there. Ned was still a little guy wearing big glasses. But he didn't look like a science teacher anymore. It must have been the gun in his hand. The one pointed right at me.

# Chapter Ten

It was a small shiny gun. It looked a bit like a toy. "Is that a real gun?" I asked.

"Oh, it's real, Charlie," said Ned. "So are the bullets that go with it."

I moved in front of Penny. Ned told me to stay still. Lindsay said, "Do what he says, Charlie. He'll use the gun if he has to."

I looked at Lindsay. "I'm guessing I won't get to drive you to the beach," I said.

"I'm sorry, Charlie," said Lindsay. "It wasn't supposed to turn out this way."

I kept my eye on Lindsay. "You stole my master key and made a copy, right?" I asked. "So your fake uncle could search for the Countess?"

"Ned told me nobody would get hurt," said Lindsay.

"But Mr. Ignato got hurt, didn't he?" I said. "Who pushed him down the stairs? You or Ned?"

"I had nothing to do with that part," said Lindsay.

"Shut up, Lindsay," said Ned. "Now where is it, Charlie?"

I heard Penny's voice behind me. "Charlie doesn't know where the Countess is," she said. "I do."

"You better tell me right now," said Ned. "Or I'm going to shoot Charlie."

"Shoot him," said Penny, still behind me. "I don't care. But if you kill Charlie, you'll never see the diamond."

"You're bluffing," said Ned. "Charlie here treats you like royalty. You hang out together all the time. You expect me to believe that you don't care if he gets killed?"

"She really doesn't," I said. "She only keeps me around to tie her shoelaces."

Ned was not convinced. "In that case, why don't you move out of the way, Charlie? There's no use in both of you getting shot."

My feet felt glued to the floor. "It's not that I don't want to do what you say," I told him. "But I'm too scared to move."

The whole thing was a lot like an episode of *Little Miss Murder*. Only I couldn't turn off the TV and walk away.

"Suit yourself," said Ned. "Too bad you'll never get your driver's license, Charlie," he added, waving the gun a little too close.

It's funny. You know what I thought at that very moment? That the next ride I took in the pig was going to be in the back, lying down.

But then Penny said, "I'll tell you where the Countess is. But you have to answer a few questions. That's fair, isn't it?"

Ned thought about this. "Okay, shoot," he said, smiling. I guess he thought he was funny.

Penny glared at Ned. And then she pointed her finger at him. It *was* just like *Little Miss Murder*! "*You're* the murderer, aren't you, Ned?" she shouted. "*You* pushed Mr. Ignato down the stairs and killed him!"

And you know what? Just like on Penny's show, Ned confessed. "It was an accident," he said. "I just wanted to know where the diamond was. I grabbed Ignato on the stairs, and he started to struggle. He even hit me with that cane of his. I lost my temper."

"And ruined everything," Lindsay told Ned. "The old man didn't even know who you were. He didn't know *either* of us. He just saw you coming out of my room. But you had to panic."

Ned told Lindsay to stay quiet or he'd keep her share of the diamond. "Like I said, it was an accident," he explained. "Even so, I should have made sure the old man was dead. But there was no time. Lucky for me, he didn't make it."

Penny said, "Sam Logan was your cellmate. That was lucky too, wasn't it, Ned? That's how you knew Mr. Ignato had the diamond."

"Sam liked to talk," said Ned. "There's not much else to do in prison. And you know what his favorite subject was, Charlie? Your pal Iggy. And his famous stolen diamond. Sam showed me letters on your hotel notepaper. And, little by little, I put most of it together."

"So why didn't you just steal the Countess and go?" I asked.

"Because I didn't know where the diamond was," said Ned. "The old man never told Sam exactly where he hid it. I discovered the safe when I searched his room. But I didn't have the combination. Then I remembered all those letters Ignato wrote to Sam."

Ned laughed. "The old man kept writing about this kid named Charlie. He said the kid was like a son to him. The only friend he had in the world besides Sam. I figured you'd lead me straight to the diamond, Charlie. All I had to do was wait."

"That's why you moved into the hotel. And pretended to be Lindsay's uncle," I said. "You wanted me to lead you to the diamond."

"Or me," said Penny. "That's why you started the fire in my room, isn't it, Ned? You figured Charlie and I were friends, right? That I might have the diamond. The fire would make me panic. And I'd take it with me, if I had it."

"I saw the matches on your bedside table. I figured it was worth the risk," said Ned. "Once the fire started? I was sure one of you would head straight for the diamond."

Ned looked at Penny like he wanted to shoot her too. "The one thing I wasn't counting on?" he said. "Charlie here cares more about you than the diamond. Can you imagine that? And you expect me to believe you're not friends?"

"We're not!" I said.

Penny looked at me and said, "*Maybe* we are." As if she wasn't sure.

"Enough talk," said Ned. "Where's the Countess?"

He looked like he was going to fire the gun. I thought about what Iggy had said. About how desperate criminals were the most dangerous. I could feel the sweat dripping down my back. "Give it to him, Penny," I said. Suddenly wishing for the days when my biggest problem was steering the pig.

"Okay," said Penny. Like she was handing over a stick of gum. "It's right here in my purse."

Ned said, "Go get it, Lindsay."

Lindsay went through Penny's purse. There was a lot of stuff in it. Dog treats, cigarettes, three pairs of sunglasses. But finally Lindsay discovered a little bag. She looked inside. And there it was. The Countess Grazelli diamond. Lindsay held it toward the light and stared at it. Like she was under some kind of spell.

Ned said, "Bring it over here." Lindsay brought the diamond to Ned. He looked at Penny and said, "You kept a million-dollar diamond in your purse? You're a lot smarter on-screen, kid."

Penny said, "You know the diamond has a curse on it, don't you, Ned?"

"I'll take my chances," said Ned. He looked at me. "How do you put up with her and the nonstop talking, Charlie? I've only been around her a couple of minutes. And I feel like breaking her other arm."

"I hope you get run over by an ice-cream truck," said Penny.

"I don't think you want anything happening to me just yet," said Ned. "We're going to take out a little insurance policy. To make sure you don't do anything foolish. Like calling the cops. Grab the dog, Lindsay."

Lindsay went over to the couch and scooped up Baby.

"No!" said Penny.

Ned kept the gun pointed at me. "Shut up, Penny," he said. "One more word out of you and I swear, Charlie will never tie another shoelace."

Lindsay looked guilty as she held Baby. She said, "We'll call you about the dog when we're safe. I promise." And then Ned, Lindsay and Baby were gone.

Tears were streaming down Penny's face. "Don't cry," I said. "They'll give Baby back. All they want is to get away with the Countess."

"You don't understand," said Penny. "I don't think they will give Baby back. Not when they discover what I've done."

"What did you do?"

"They don't have the Countess. The diamond I gave them? It was a fake."

# Chapter Eleven

"A fake!" I said. "What do you mean?"

"I mean it's not a real diamond," said Penny. "The prop man on our show is a friend of mine. I asked him to make it for me. It's made of *glass*, Charlie."

"But it looked so real," I said. "I couldn't tell the difference."

"I figured Ned wouldn't either," said Penny. "How many people have seen a real diamond that big?

Besides, I don't know if you've noticed, but Ned isn't exactly a criminal mastermind. But now I'm not so sure. Sooner or later one of them is bound to discover the diamond is a fake." She held back a sob. "They wouldn't hurt Baby, would they, Hopeless?"

I wasn't sure. But I didn't want Penny to know that. "All they want is the Countess," I said. "As long as we have the diamond, Baby will be safe."

"But what are we going to do?" asked Penny. "Baby gets upset around strangers. It takes her a long time to trust people. Besides me, you're the only person she lets feed her."

"She'll eat when she gets hungry enough," I said.

"Baby's very stubborn," said Penny. "She'd rather starve than eat store-bought dog food. And she doesn't have her special pillow. What if they make her sleep on the cold floor?"

"Don't panic," I said. "Baby is braver than she looks."

"No, she isn't," said Penny. "Baby's like me. She's too used to getting what she wants. I hope they don't take her for a drive. She gets carsick unless I sing to her. I've messed up, haven't I, Hopeless?"

She looked so sad. I didn't know what to say.

"Why did you do it, anyway?" she asked. "Why did you stand in front of me when Ned had the gun?"

"I don't know," I said. "I just did."

"Nobody's ever done that for me, Charlie." Penny started to say something else. Then she stopped.

"Where's the real diamond?" I asked.

Penny used her good arm to wipe away a few tears. "You're not going to like it," she said. "Promise you won't yell at me?"

"I promise," I said.

Penny looked down at her broken arm. "The Countess is inside my cast."

"*Inside* your cast?" I said. "How can it be inside your cast?"

"Well, my arm isn't exactly broken," said Penny. "In fact, it's not broken at all."

That's when Penny showed me how she could pull apart her cast. With a little effort, she split the cast evenly into two separate and identical pieces. Each long piece ran down opposite sides of her arm. From just above the elbow to the knuckles of her fingers.

Both sections could easily snap back together. Once in place they fit around Penny's healthy arm as snugly as two matching pieces in a jigsaw puzzle. They looked exactly like a regular plaster cast.

I couldn't believe it. "How did you do that?" I asked.

"I told you the prop man is a friend of mine, Hopeless," said Penny. "The cast is only a prop. Like the fake diamond I gave to Ned. We use stuff like this on the show all the time."

"But why would you fake having a broken arm?" I asked.

"I needed a good excuse to be off the show while Lou bargained for a new contract."

I kept staring at Penny's arm. Now free of the fake cast and perfectly fine. "Why didn't you tell me your arm wasn't broken?" I asked.

"Because I am a serious actor," said Penny. "And I was playing the part of someone with a broken arm. Besides, if it ever got out that I was just pretending? The reporters would get the story and ruin my career. I couldn't risk you telling someone else."

"You know what I think?" I said. "You liked having me as your personal slave. Dicing your carrots. Tying your shoelaces. And lighting your stupid French cigarettes. And it was all for nothing!"

"You promised you wouldn't yell, Hopeless," said Penny.

"I'm not yelling!" I said. She was so good at making me mad. That's when I remembered the diamond. "Let's see the Countess, Penny."

Penny showed me the bottom half of her fake cast. Inside was a little drawstring bag tucked neatly into a square compartment molded into the cast. "This is where I used to hide my emergency pack of cigarettes," said Penny.

"So that's why I could never find them all," I said.

"And that's why you could never find the Countess," said Penny. "It was right here all along."

Penny took the bag out of its secret hiding place. Then she took the Countess out of the bag. I watched it sparkle as she held it in her hand. "This is the real diamond, Hopeless," she said. "I wanted to keep it so badly. Now I just want Baby back."

"You expect me to give up my share of a million-dollar diamond?" I asked. "Just to save your dog?"

"The diamond doesn't even belong to us, Hopeless," said Penny. "Anyway, you never wanted it in the first place. Plus there's another reason."

"What's that?" I asked.

"I need your help," said Penny. "And you're the only friend I've got."

I wanted to correct Penny Price and tell her that I wasn't her friend. But for some reason, I couldn't do it.

Then I thought of Baby. And of the tears that had streamed down Penny's face as Lindsay took her away.

"Okay, Penny," I said. "I'll help you get Baby back."

"So what do we do next?" asked Penny.

"Wait for their phone call," I said. "It won't be long. Either Baby will drive them crazy or they'll find out the truth. About the fake diamond."

Penny looked afraid. "What if Ned decides to come back here tonight?" she asked. "They still have a copy of the master key."

"Don't worry about that," I said.

That night I sat outside Penny's room with the fire extinguisher. In case I had to put out another fire.

Sitting in a chair outside Penny's room, I thought about a lot of things. I thought of Mr. Ignato lying at the bottom of the stairs. I thought of Baby without her special pillow. And I thought of Penny on the other side of the door. Afraid to go to sleep.

The last thing I remember thinking? That maybe Penny was my friend after all. Whether I liked it or not.

Then I fell asleep. And dreamed about Ned pointing a gun at me outside Penny's room. In the dream I tried to spray Ned with the fire extinguisher. But the fire extinguisher wouldn't spray. Dream Ned just smiled at me. "I love the Hotel Hopeless," he said. "Nothing ever works."

And then Dream Ned shot me.

# Chapter Twelve

We got the call from Ned and Lindsay the next morning. They had figured it out. Ned was angry. "I want the real Countess now, Charlie," he said. "You've got half an hour. Or the dog is dead."

Ned and Lindsay wanted us to meet them. At a deserted warehouse just outside of town. I wanted to call a cab. But Penny was too worried about Baby to wait. "We'll never make it to that warehouse in half an hour," she said. "There isn't enough time."

Then Penny saw the pig parked behind the hotel. She grabbed the bag with the Countess in it. "You told me your friend Dexter always leaves his keys in the car, remember? Let's go, Hopeless. You're driving that hearse!"

Dexter still wasn't talking to me. And I didn't think driving his car without an official license would make things better. "Me, drive the pig?" I said to Penny. "Dexter just got his old limo job back. I'll wreck his car *twice*."

"It's an emergency, Hopeless," said Penny. "Either you're driving that car or *I* am!"

"But you can't even see over the wheel," I said.

"So what?" she said. "I drove a golf cart once. It's the same thing, isn't it?"

I was too stunned to answer.

Penny stomped her foot. "Are you my friend or not, Hopeless?"

I didn't know how to answer that question. "Okay, but I'm driving," I said.

I was hoping Dexter had kept the pig locked for once. But the door wasn't locked. So we got in the car and took off.

I didn't think I could drive that fast. But soon I was dodging in and out of traffic. Cars were whizzing by so fast it felt like I was flying a plane.

I tried to remember everything Dexter had taught me. And I thought I was doing pretty good until I saw Dexter's face pop up in the rearview mirror.

His hair was all messed up, and he looked groggy. He must have been taking a nap in the back of the pig.

Then we hit a bump, and Dexter was wide awake. "Charlie, please tell me I'm still dreaming!" he yelled. "Tell me you are *not* speeding through the city without a license. Because if you were, do you know what I would have to say? 'You are going to kill us! Also, you will wreck the pig!'"

I tried to explain why Penny and I had stolen the hearse. But it was hard to talk and concentrate on the road at the same time. Horns were honking. Dexter kept yelling at me to stop. Until he noticed Penny in the passenger seat. "Hey, it's Trixie Tucker!" he said. "I mean, it's Penny Price."

I swerved to avoid a squirrel, and the tires squealed. But Dexter didn't seem to mind at all. He just kept staring at Penny.

"No cast, huh?" Dexter said to Penny. "Your arm's all better now?"

"It's a long story," said Penny. She took a cigarette out of her purse and lit it. I swerved to avoid a pigeon. What was with all the potential roadkill? "There is no smoking in the pig," I said.

"Penny Price can smoke in the pig anytime," said Dexter with a goofy grin. Then he looked at the speedometer. "Hey, Charlie," he said. "You better slow down. We don't want the police chasing us."

"Actually, that wouldn't be such a bad idea," I said.

Penny explained our situation to Dexter. "Maybe we should pull over so I can drive," he said.

Penny shook her head. "We're almost there. Besides, Hopeless is doing great."

"Yeah, I guess he is," said Dexter. To my surprise, I could hear a bit of pride in his voice. "Just try not to sweat on the seat too much, Charlie." He turned to Penny. "They are genuine leather."

We were getting closer to the warehouse. That's when I got the idea for Dexter to call the police to tell them that someone had stolen his hearse.

"Let's call some reporters too," said Penny. "They'll probably get here faster than the police."

We were all pretty excited. It was almost like we were having fun. Then we remembered who was waiting for us at the warehouse. Everything got quiet after that.

I asked Penny to give me the Countess. And she handed it over without a word. We told Dexter to wait in the pig and watch for the police. He wanted to come with us. But Penny told him he had a very important job. "We might have to make a quick getaway," she said. "Stay here and keep the motor running."

The warehouse was big and dark. But Ned's shiny little gun caught the light before we saw him. Ned had Baby in his arms. The gun was pointed right at her head. "The diamond, Charlie," he said. "Right now. No tricks."

I took the little bag out of my pocket and showed Ned the diamond. Then I put the Countess back in the bag and threw it across the floor. It landed close to Ned's feet. "Get it, Lindsay," he said. Lindsay came out of the shadows to grab the diamond. I thought it was all over.

But then Baby jumped out of Ned's arms, grabbing the bag with her teeth. She took off into the dark. Ned aimed the gun at Baby. A shot rang out as Penny pushed Ned. The bullet just missed the dog.

Ned pushed back at Penny. She fell hard on the cement floor, crying out in pain. Ned ran off after Baby.

Maybe it was seeing Penny on the floor, unable to get up. Maybe it reminded me of Mr. Ignato lying at the bottom of the hotel stairs. Whatever it was, it made me stop feeling scared. I got angry. Angry enough to race after Ned, tackle him and wrestle him to the floor.

The gun went off when I was trying to get it away from Ned. But it didn't hit anything. So I just kept hitting his gun hand against the cement until he let go. The next thing I remember is the police running into the warehouse. It took a while to sort everything out.

We found Baby in a corner of the warehouse. With the bag still in her teeth. She dropped the bag in front of Penny. But Penny couldn't pick it up. Her arm was broken for real this time.

Dexter took Penny and Baby to the hospital in the pig. The rest of us went down to the police station. Including the Countess. By that time there was a bunch of reporters outside the hospital, crowded around Dexter's hearse.

The reporters were taking pictures and shouting at Penny. Asking what was going on. Dexter told me Penny was in a lot of pain. "But you know the funny thing?" said Dexter. "She was smiling! Like she was actually happy."

Pretty soon everyone heard about how Penny had solved a real murder. Now she had more admirers than ever. The producers of her show signed her to a new contract with way more money. Ned and Lindsay went to jail. And we turned the Countess over to the Italian government.

The best part? There was a big reward for the

return of the diamond. My mother was able to pay down the mortgage and keep the hotel.

Even though Penny is back working on *Little Miss Murder* and can live wherever she wants now, she still hasn't moved out of the Hotel Hope. She had enough money from her share of the reward to hire Dexter as her personal chauffeur. He tried it out but quit about two weeks later. "The funeral business is way less stressful," he explained. I told him I understood. And just like that, we were best friends again.

Somehow I managed to pass my driver's test. I even bought a beat-up old car that someone painted pink. Dexter named it the piglet. I do not let Penny smoke in the piglet.

I am still slicing Baby's steak and tying Penny's shoelaces. But Penny's cast will be off soon. Yesterday it was nice and sunny. We were driving to the beach, enjoying the quiet. And Penny said,

"Thank you, Charlie Hope." She didn't say for what. And I didn't ask. But I've noticed that she doesn't call me Hopeless anymore.

Sometimes when Penny is in the car with me, I think of my friend Iggy. And how I promised to forgive him for cursing me with the Countess. I think of all the things that happened. Like wrecking the pig, and the fire in Penny's room. About how Lindsay only pretended to like me. And how Ned's greed made him hate everybody. Even himself.

And then I'll roll down the window of the piglet. And feel the breeze drifting in. Penny will say, "Take me home, Charlie." I know that she means the Hotel Hope.

That's when I remember there's nothing to forgive. Nothing at all.